To Peter Orton, with love and appreciation   KH and HC

Published by Pleasant Company Publications
© 2002 HIT Entertainment PLC
Text copyright © 2002 Katharine Holabird
Illustrations copyright © 2002 Helen Craig

Visit our Web site at **www.americangirl.com** and Angelina's
very own site at **www.angelinaballerina.com**

Printed in Italy
02 03 04 05 06 07 08 09 LEGO 10 9 8 7 6 5 4 3 2 1

A catalog of record for this book is available from the Library of Congress.

Angelina and Henry

Story by **Katharine Holabird** Illustrations by **Helen Craig**

PLEASANT COMPANY PUBLICATIONS™

Angelina could hardly wait to go camping
in the Big Cat Mountains with Uncle Louie.
"I'll dance under the stars," she smiled
as she spun around the room.

Little cousin Henry showed off his panama hat.
"I'm going to be a great explorer," he announced.

"Are you fit and fearless?" Uncle Louie asked
with a wink. "Big Cat could still be up there."

They set off early the next morning, with Mrs. Mouseling's cheese crumpets still warm in their pockets.

At first, Angelina skipped and twirled along the winding trail. Then she noticed Uncle Louie disappearing up the mountain and had to race to catch up.

As they climbed higher and higher, Angelina began to feel very hot and tired.

Henry happily jogged ahead of her. "You're too slow, Angelina!" he teased. "Big Cat will get you."

"My backpack is so heavy," moaned Angelina.

"Only another mile or two to go," Uncle Louie encouraged her.

At last they reached the top of the mountain, and Angelina collapsed with a sigh.

"We've got to set up camp before sunset," said Uncle Louie, showing Angelina and Henry how to unpack.

"Can we have our campfire now?" Angelina asked hopefully.

"You'll need to collect some wood," Uncle Louie replied, "while I put up the tents."

Henry scampered off into the trees. "Let's explore!" he shouted, waving a stick.

"We have to get the firewood first," Angelina reminded him.

But it was much more fun exploring, and soon the two little mouselings were deep in the forest.

They played hide-and-seek and sword fighting, and then they discovered a secret fort.
Before long they'd forgotten all about Uncle Louie and collecting firewood.

When they finally stopped to look around, the forest was growing dark and shadowy. The wind was beginning to whistle, and strange shapes loomed behind the trees.

Henry dropped his stick. "I'm hungry," he whimpered.

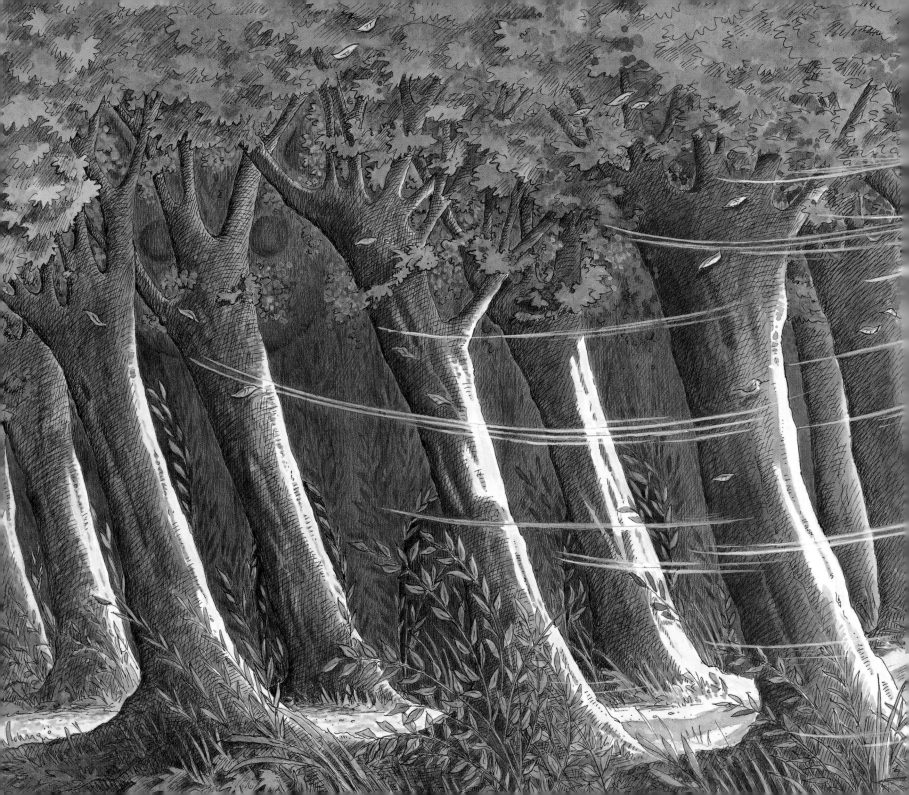

Meeeeow! Something howled behind them.

"What's that?" Henry squeaked. He grabbed Angelina's tail.

Two large ears twitched behind a tree.

"It's just a shadow," whispered Angelina, pulling Henry into the fort.

A black tail flashed by in the wind.

"Big Cat's coming!" wailed Henry, hiding his eyes.

"We'll just have to be brave," said Angelina, and she leaped out into the dark night. "Shoo! Shooo! Shoooooo!" she shouted, waving her sword.

Rain pelted down and thunder roared. Then lightning struck, and a big branch crashed to the ground.

Big Cat vanished.

Poor Henry's whiskers were trembling. Angelina held him close, and while the storm raged around them, she made up songs and silly jokes to comfort him.

Finally the wild winds passed. Angelina was soaking wet, but she'd kept Henry cozy and warm. She gathered him up and set off through the woods, calling for Uncle Louie.

Suddenly Angelina stopped. Two yellow eyes were glinting through the trees…

"Angelina! Henry! Thank goodness you're safe."

It was Uncle Louie with two lanterns. He hugged the little mouselings and then carried Henry to the campsite with Angelina lighting the way.

They all made the bonfire together and had a great feast of chestnuts and cheddarburgers. Angelina and Henry promised Uncle Louie they'd never run off again, and they told him all about their scary adventure.

After supper, Uncle Louie played tunes on his concertina, while Angelina and Henry danced around the campfire.

Before bedtime, they sat out under the stars.

"I lost my panama hat," Henry said sadly.
"But we really scared off old Big Cat, didn't we?"

"Yes," Angelina agreed. "And that's because we're
both fit and fearless explorers."

A free catalogue for your little ballerina!

If you've fallen in love with Angelina Ballerina,™ you'll love the American Girl® catalogue. Angelina's world comes to life in a line of charming playthings and girl-sized clothes that complement her beautiful books. You'll also discover Bitty Baby,® a precious baby doll with her own adorable clothes and accessories.

To receive your free catalogue, return this card, visit our Web site at **americangirl.com**, or call **1-800-845-0005.**

Send me a catalogue:

Name _____ Girl's birth date __/__/__

Address _____

City _____ State ___ Zip ___

(___) _____
Phone ❏ Home ❏ Work

86945i

Send my friend a catalogue:

Name _____

Address _____

City _____ State ___ Zip ___

86947i

American Girl®

PO BOX 620497
MIDDLETON WI 53562-0497